Randy Johnson
and the ARIZONA DIAMONDBACKS
2001 WORLD SERIES

by Michael Sandler

Consultant: Jim Sherman
Head Baseball Coach
University of Delaware

BALDWIN PUBLIC LIBRARY

BEARPORT
PUBLISHING

New York, New York

Credits

Cover and Title Page, © Mike Fiala/AFP/Getty Images; 4, © Mike Fiala/AFP/Getty Images; 5, © John Biever/SI/Icon SMI; 6, © Livermore High School; 7, © Courtesy of University of Southern California; 8, © Ronald C. Modra/Sports Imagery/Getty Images; 9, © AP Images/Timothy Fitzgerald; 10, © Doug Pensinger/Getty Images; 11, © AP Images/Thearon Henderson; 12, © Monica M. Davey/AFP/Getty Images; 13, © Jeff Gross/ALLSPORT/Getty Images; 14, © Harry How/ALLSPORT/Getty Images; 15, © REUTERS/Shaun Best; 16, © Jeff Gross/ALLSPORT/Getty Images; 17, © AP Images/Joe Cavaretta; 18, © REUTERS/Mike Segar; 19, © REUTERS/Mike Segar; 20, © AP Images/John Bazemore; 21, © Jed Jacobsohn/ALLSPORT/Getty Images; 22T, © REUTERS/Colin Braley; 22C, © AP Images/Roy Dabner; 22B, © Harry How/ALLSPORT/Getty Images.

Publisher: Kenn Goin
Senior Editor: Lisa Wiseman
Creative Director: Spencer Brinker
Design: Stacey May
Photo Researcher: Omni-Photo Communications, Inc.

Library of Congress Cataloging-in-Publication Data

Sandler, Michael.
 Randy Johnson and the Arizona Diamondbacks : 2001 World Series / by Michael Sandler.
     p. cm. — (World series superstars)
 Includes bibliographical references and index.
 ISBN-13: 978-1-59716-638-6 (library binding)
 ISBN-10: 1-59716-638-3 (library binding)
 1. Johnson, Randy, 1963- 2. Baseball players—United States—Biography—Juvenile literature. 3. Anaheim Angels (Baseball team) —Juvenile literature. 4. Arizona Diamondbacks (Baseball team) —Juvenile literature. 5. World Series (Baseball) (2001) —Juvenile literature. I. Title.

GV865.J599S36 2008
796.357092—dc22
(B)
 2007031360

Copyright © 2008 Bearport Publishing Company, Inc. All rights reserved. No part of this publication may be reproduced in whole or in part, stored in a retrieval system, or transmitted in any form or by any means, electronic, mechanical, photocopying, recording, or otherwise, without written permission from the publisher.

For more information, write to Bearport Publishing Company, Inc., 101 Fifth Avenue, Suite 6R, New York, New York 10003. Printed in the United States of America.

10 9 8 7 6 5 4 3 2 1

★ Contents ★

Pitching Relief............................ 4
Practicing Pitches....................... 6
The Big Unit............................... 8
Arriving in Arizona..................... 10
The 2001 Season....................... 12
The Mighty Yankees.................... 14
Randy to the Rescue.................. 16
Game 7..................................... 18
The Final Inning......................... 20

Key Players................................ 22
Glossary.................................... 23
Bibliography.............................. 24
Read More................................. 24
Learn More Online...................... 24
Index.. 24

Pitching Relief

Randy Johnson had always been a **starter**. Now, during Game 7 of the 2001 World Series, the Arizona Diamondbacks needed him to pitch in **relief**.

The Diamondbacks had no choice. They had to stop the New York Yankees. Otherwise, they would lose the series.

Randy walked to the mound. Reliever or starter, he didn't care. This was the chance he'd been waiting for.

Alfonso Soriano's eighth inning homer gave New York the lead in Game 7 of the 2001 World Series.

Randy in action during Game 7

Throughout his **career**, Randy had started nearly 400 games. He had pitched in relief only a few times.

Practicing Pitches

Pitching had always been Randy's first love. As a kid, he practiced by throwing balls at the garage door of his family's home. Over and over, he aimed at a **strike zone** taped to the door.

Even when he was young, his arm was very strong. His height was impressive, too. By high school, Randy was well over six feet (1.83 m) tall. Batters worried whenever they saw Randy on the mound.

In high school, Randy (#44) played both baseball and basketball.

After high school, Randy pitched for the University of Southern California.

The Big Unit

Randy made it to the **major leagues** in 1988. Over the next 10 seasons, he grew stronger and stronger.

His 100-mile-per-hour (161-k-p-h) fastball was nearly impossible to hit. Often he led the league in **strikeouts**. In 1995, he won the American League **Cy Young Award**.

Still, Randy's heart was set on a bigger prize. "My dream is to win a World Series, not the Cy Young," he said.

Randy got his major league start with the Montreal Expos.

Randy also played for the Seattle Mariners and the Houston Astros before joining the Diamondbacks.

Randy is nicknamed "The Big Unit." At 6'10" (2.08 m), he is the tallest pitcher in major league history.

Arriving in Arizona

In 1999, Randy joined the Arizona Diamondbacks. Few believed he would get his **title** with this team.

The Diamondbacks were a brand-new team. They had played their first game only a year before. New teams usually didn't get to the World Series. It took years to build up enough talent.

Arizona, however, played surprisingly well in Randy's first year. The Big Unit was one of the reasons. He won 17 games and struck out 364 batters.

Randy throwing one of his impossible-to-hit pitches

Randy (#51) celebrates a win with his teammates.

Arizona won 100 games in Randy's first season with the team.

The 2001 Season

In Randy's third season with the Diamondbacks, the team really took off. Led by Randy and another strikeout king, Curt Schilling, Arizona grabbed the **division** title. In the **playoffs**, they rolled right over the St. Louis Cardinals and the Atlanta Braves.

Randy and Curt were simply too tough for their **opponents**. Against the Cardinals and the Braves, Randy and Curt started six games in total. Arizona won five of them. They were headed to the World Series.

Curt Schilling on the mound

Randy after striking out a batter during the playoffs

Randy reached 3,000 career strikeouts faster than any pitcher in major league history.

The Mighty Yankees

Arizona's job, however, was about to get harder. Their opponents, the New York Yankees, never seemed to lose.

The Yankees had won three straight World Series. Even Randy and Curt would have a tough time with big hitters such as Derek Jeter and Bernie Williams.

Fans were shocked when Arizona won the first two games. Then the Yankees came to life, winning three in a row. One more win would give New York the title.

Randy's fans count his strikeouts (K's) during Game 2 of the 2001 World Series.

Derek Jeter's homer won Game 4 for the Yankees.

As of 2001, the Yankees had won 26 World Series titles.

Randy to the Rescue

If Arizona lost another game, the series would be over. The team turned to Randy to save them. As usual, the Big Unit came through. In Game 6, he held New York to just two runs.

While Randy did his magic on the mound, his teammates exploded at the plate. Their 22 hits set a World Series record. The Diamondbacks roared to a 15-2 victory. The 2001 Series was going to a **winner-take-all** seventh game.

Once again, Randy came through with a win for the Diamondbacks.

In Game 6, Randy even got a hit.

The 15-2 loss was the worst **defeat** in Yankees playoff history. In 293 games, no team had ever beaten New York so badly.

Game 7

In Game 7, Arizona started Curt. The Yankees **countered** with their best pitcher—20-game winner Roger Clemens.

The two ace pitchers kept hitters off of the bases. After seven innings, the game was tied, 1-1. Then the Yankees' Alfonso Soriano hit a home run.

Down 2-1, Curt was taken out of the game. Arizona turned to Randy once again. Even though he had started the night before, he wasn't tired. The Big Unit came in and shut down the Yankees' hitters.

Alfonso Soriano hits a home run off of Curt Schilling.

Randy didn't give up any hits in his relief appearance.

An unhappy Curt in the dugout during Game 7

19

The Final Inning

Randy's pitching was amazing, but Arizona was still losing. It was the bottom of the ninth. Three Arizona outs and the series would be over.

To make things worse for Arizona, Mariano Rivera was on the mound. The Yankees' reliever was almost unhittable.

However, Mariano couldn't stop the Diamondbacks. Tony Womack slapped a double to bring in the tying run. Then Luis Gonzalez knocked home the winning run.

Arizona had beaten the powerful Yankees. The Big Unit had his title!

Luis Gonzalez celebrates his game-winning hit.

After the game, Randy and Curt were named co-MVPs (Most Valuable Players) of the 2001 World Series.

21

Key Players

Randy, along with some other key players, helped the Arizona Diamondbacks win the 2001 World Series.

Tony Womack #5

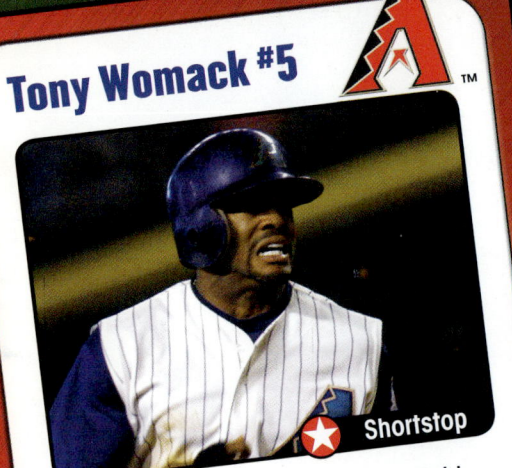

Shortstop

- **Bats:** Left
- **Throws:** Right
- **Born:** 9/25/1969 in Danville, Virginia
- **Height:** 5'9" (1.75 m)
- **Weight:** 170 pounds (77 kg)

Series Highlight
Doubled to knock in the tying run in Game 7

Randy Johnson #51

Starting Pitcher

- **Bats:** Right
- **Throws:** Left
- **Born:** 9/10/1963 in Walnut Creek, California
- **Height:** 6'10" (2.08 m)
- **Weight:** 225 pounds (102 kg)

Series Highlights
Won Games 2, 6, and 7 for Arizona

Curt Schilling #38

Starting Pitcher

- **Bats:** Right
- **Throws:** Right
- **Born:** 11/14/1966 in Anchorage, Alaska
- **Height:** 6'5" (1.96 m)
- **Weight:** 235 pounds (107 kg)

Series Highlight
Won Game 1 for Arizona

Glossary

career (kuh-RIHR) the job a person has for a long period of time

countered (KOUN-turd) fought back

Cy Young Award (SYE YUHNG uh-WARD) an award given yearly to the best pitchers in the American and National Leagues

defeat (di-FEET) a loss

division (di-VIZH-uhn) a group of teams that compete against one another for a playoff spot

major leagues (MAY-jur LEEGZ) the highest level of professional baseball teams in the United States, made up of the American League and the National League

opponents (uh-POH-nuhnts) teams or athletes who others play against in a sporting event

playoffs (PLAY-awfss) games held after the regular season to determine who will play in the World Series

relief (ri-LEEF) when a pitcher comes into a game, after it has begun, to replace another pitcher

starter (START-ur) a pitcher who plays at the beginning of a game

strike zone (STRIKE ZOHN) the area where a ball thrown by a pitcher will be called a strike

strikeouts (STRIKE-outs) when batters swing and miss three pitches or when the umpire calls batters out after the third strike is thrown

title (TYE-tuhl) the championship; in baseball, a World Series win

winner-take-all (WIN-ur-TAYKE-AWL) a single game that decides which team will win a title

Bibliography

Christopher, Matt. *On the Mound with Randy Johnson*. New York: Little, Brown (1998).

The Arizona Republic

The New York Times

Sports Illustrated

Read More

Darraj, Susan Muaddi, and Rob Maaddi. *Randy Johnson*. New York: Chelsea House (2007).

DK Publishing. *World Series*. New York: DK Children (2004).

Zuehlke, Jeffrey. *Curt Schilling (Amazing Athletes)*. Minneapolis, MN: Lerner (2007).

Learn More Online

To learn more about Randy Johnson, the Arizona Diamondbacks, and the World Series, visit www.bearportpublishing.com/WorldSeriesSuperstars

Index

Atlanta Braves 12
Clemens, Roger 18
Cy Young Award 8
Gonzalez, Luis 20
height 6, 9
Houston Astros 9
Jeter, Derek 14–15
high school 6–7
Montreal Expos 8

New York Yankees 4, 14–15, 16–17, 18, 20
playoffs 12, 17
relief pitching 4–5, 18–19
Rivera, Mariano 20
St. Louis Cardinals 12
Schilling, Curt 12, 14, 18–19, 21, 22

Seattle Mariners 9
Soriano, Alfonso 4, 18
strikeouts 8, 10, 12–13, 14
Williams, Bernie 14
Womack, Tony 20, 22

NO LONGER THE PROPERTY OF
BALDWIN PUBLIC LIBRARY